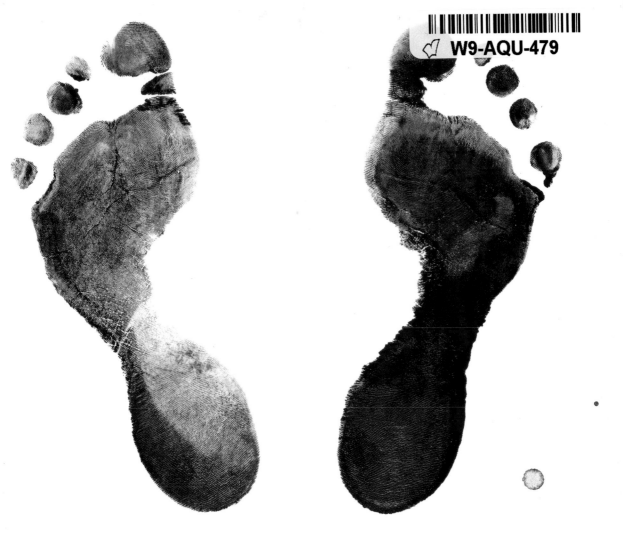

Jake's feet

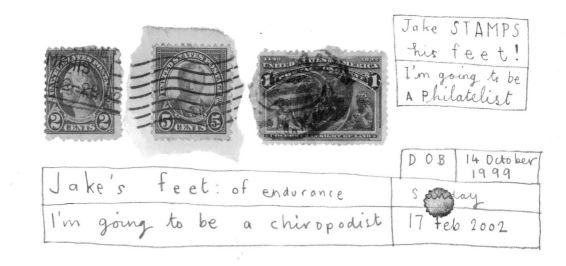

Jake STAMPS his feet! I'm going to be A Philatelist

| | DOB | 14 October 1999 |
|---|---|---|
| Jake's feet: of endurance | Sunday | |
| I'm going to be a chiropodist | 17 feb 2002 | |

12 inches = 1 foot
3 feet = 1 yard. → PRACTICE BASKETBALL in your backyard.

1 2 3 4

3B

Blue
HB

2B

Red HB

B

2B

HB

# GROW UP

## Sandy Turner

Joanna Cotler Books
An Imprint of HarperCollins
PUBLISHERS

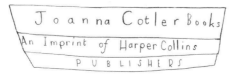

Grow Up   Copyright © 2003 by Sandy Turner
Manufactured in China. All rights reserved.
www.harperchildrens.com   Library of Congress
Cataloging-in-Publication Data   Turner, Sandy.   Grow
up / Sandy Turner.   p.   cm.   Summary: A young boy
imagines many possibilities when asked what he wants
to be when he grows up.   ISBN 0-06-000953-5 — ISBN
0-06-000954-3 (lib. bdg.)   [1. Occupations—Fiction.]
1. Title.   PZ7.T8577 Gr 2003   2001051546   [E]—dc21
1 2 3 4 5 6 7 8 9 10 ❖ First Edition

I'M going to be GREEN - FINGERED: (a gardener)

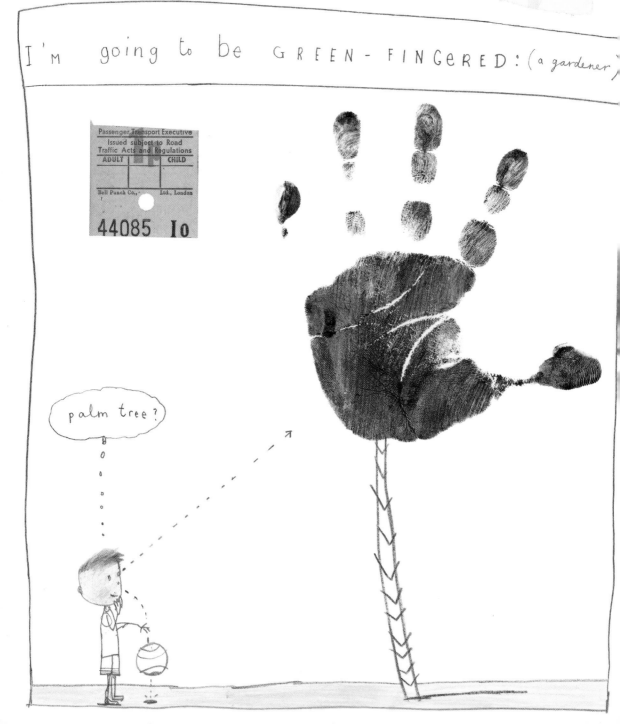

START

FINISH

FOR BILL

 and ELEANOR and LYDIA and BLANCHe  x
not forgetting Jake

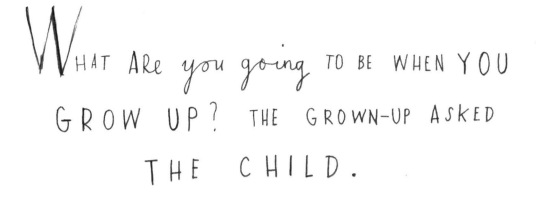

WHAT ARE you going TO BE WHEN YOU GROW UP? THE GROWN-UP ASKED THE CHILD.

I don't know,

said the CHILD . . . A NURSE ?

ooh . . . I know
I'm going to be a . . .

I'm going to be a
SCIENTIST

I'm going to be a
DENTIST

I'M GOING TO BE A
HYPNOTIST

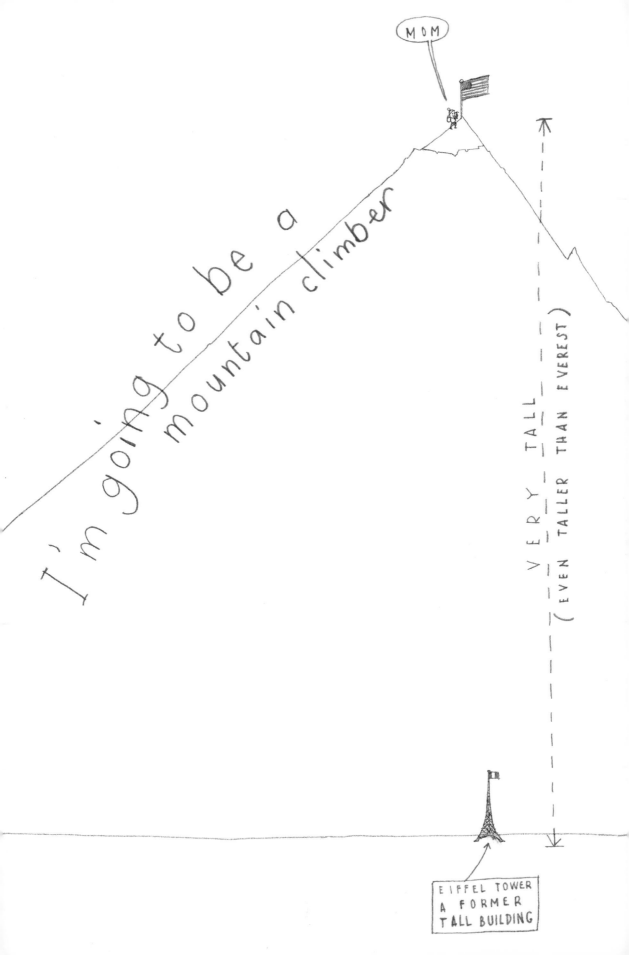

OR I MIGHT BE
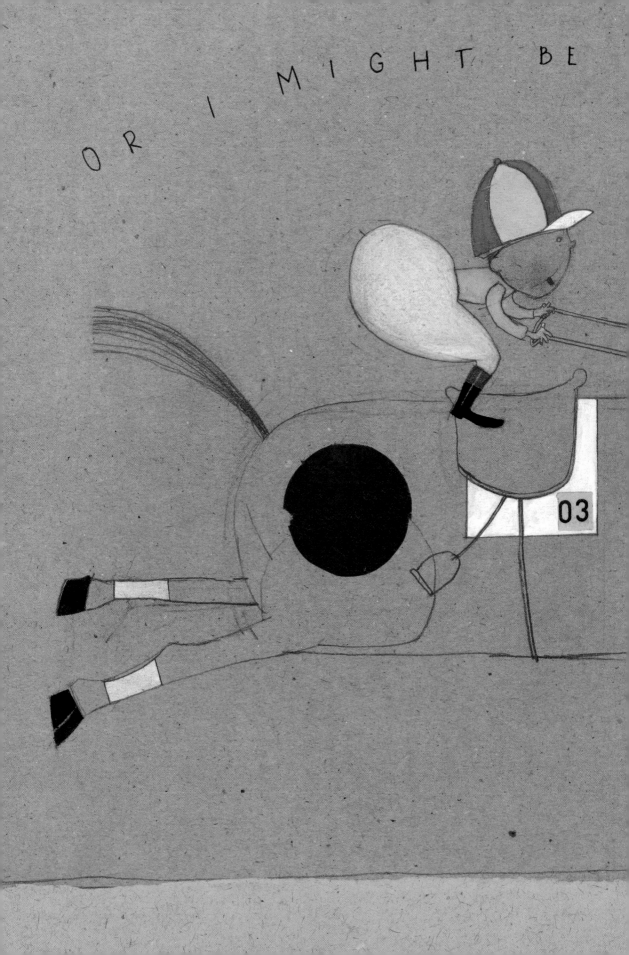

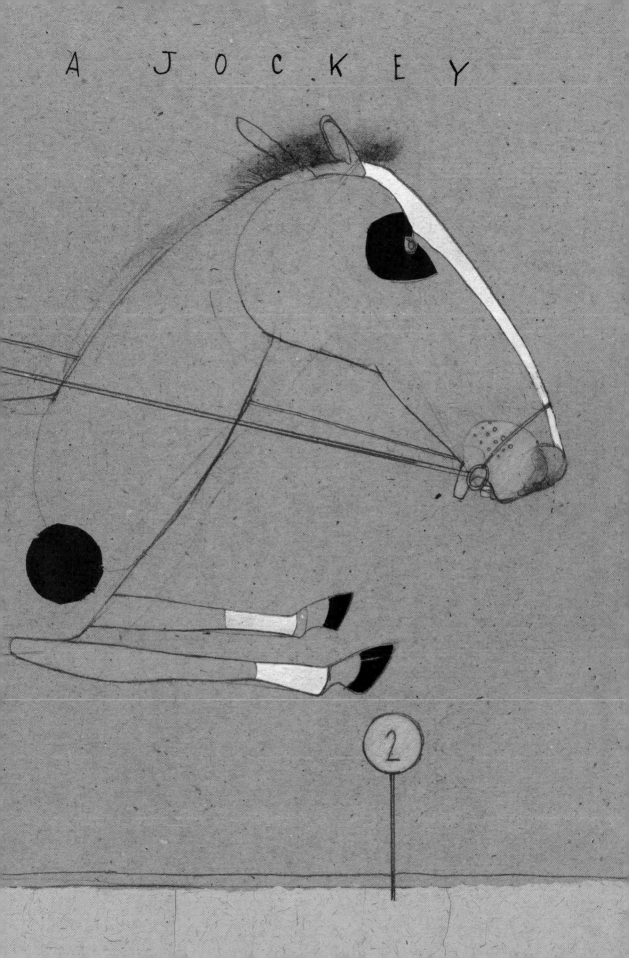

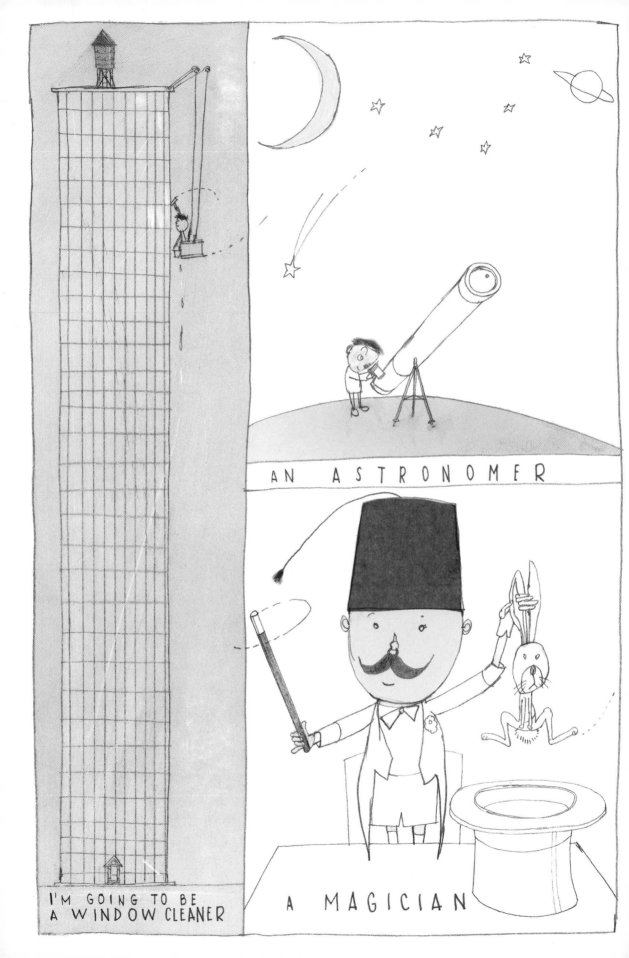

AN ASTRONOMER

A MAGICIAN

I'M GOING TO BE
A WINDOW CLEANER

OR EVEN A LION TAMER

OR A TICKET COLLECTOR

I'm going to play the SAXOPHONE

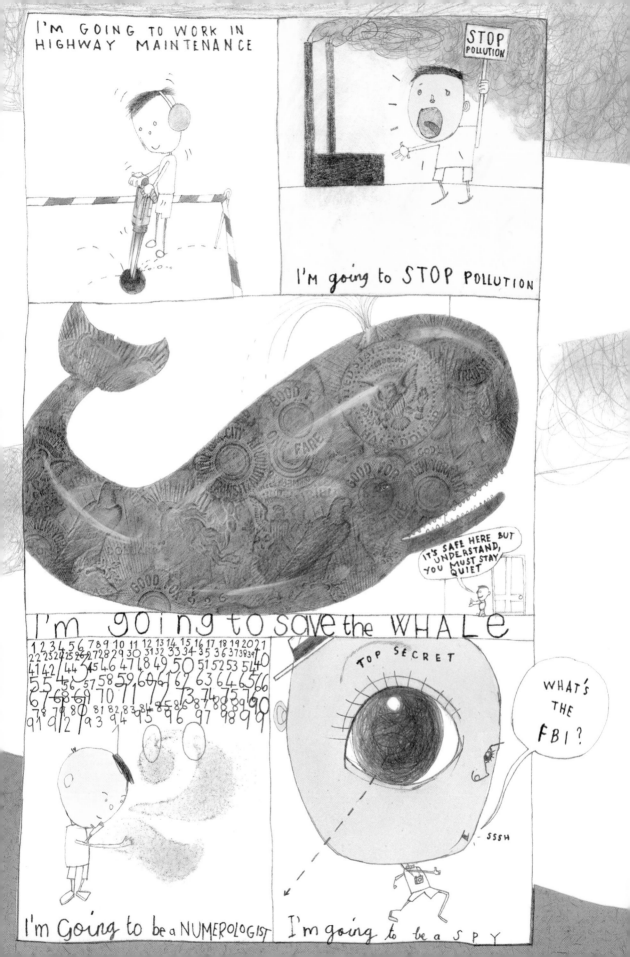

I might be a LIGHTHOUSE KEEPER

I'm going to deliver the U.S. mail.

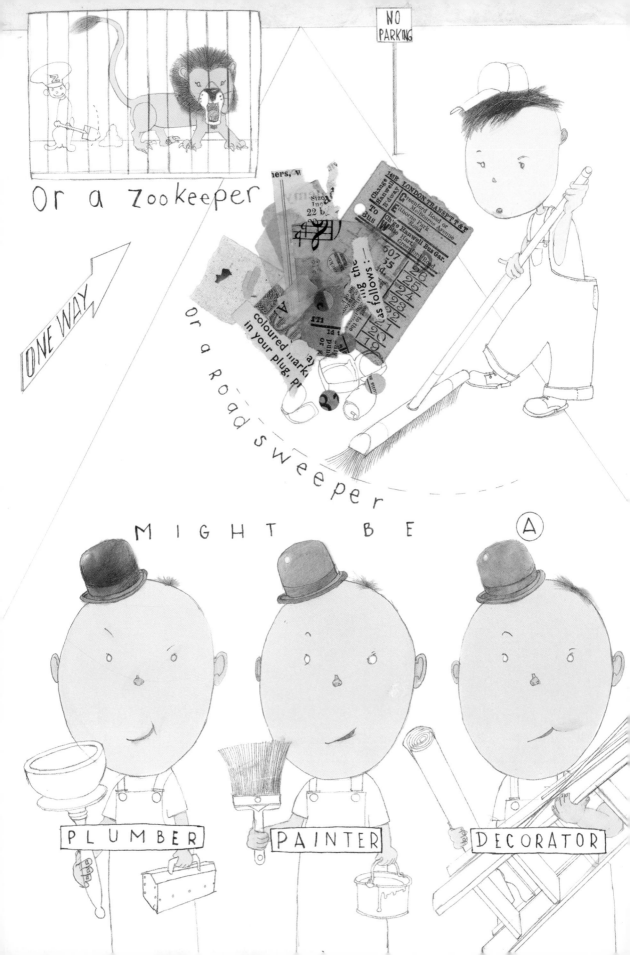

Or a zookeeper

ONE WAY

NO PARKING

Or a road sweeper

MIGHT BE A

PLUMBER

PAINTER

DECORATOR

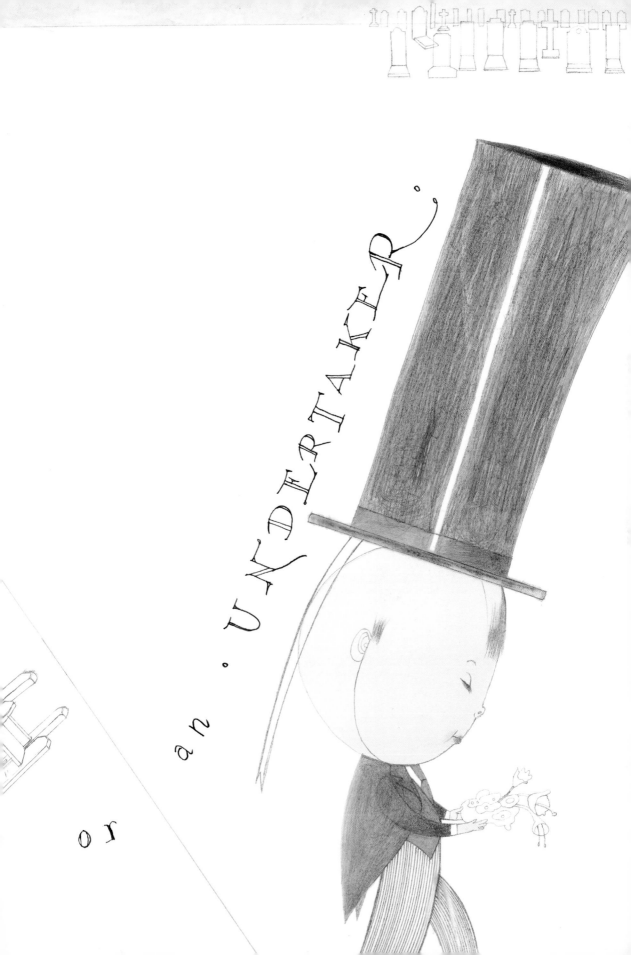

or

an · UNDERTAKER ·

I might be

Could work on a FERRY
going to be an ARCHITECT:
OR I might fly a JET

I'm going to COMMAND A FLEET of SUBMARINES

and FRO

BATTERIES NOT INCLUDED

I'm going to grow

TALLER

I am going to be the

7' 7"

# BASKETBALLER.

And the grown-up said YOU HAD better EAT UP your GREENS.

How To be an ARTIST:
<u>draw around your hand.</u>
place hand palm side down on the paper. Spread
your fingers evenly. Carefully ~~draw~~ draw round the
edges. Like tracing. Lift your hand away
an' bINGO there is an actual outline of your
HAND.    Add detail, color in.

4

5

3

2

BIG Hand

1

START

older

HANDSome